For Iona

The Tale of the Turnip
is a traditional English tale retold by Brian Alderson.

Text copyright © 1999 by Brian Alderson
Illustrations copyright © 1999 by Fritz Wegner

First U.S. edition 1999

Library of Congress Cataloging-in-Publication Data is available.

Library of Congress Catalog Card Number 98-35831

ISBN 0-7636-0494-1

2 4 6 8 10 9 7 5 3 1

Printed in Hong Kong

This book was typeset in Opti Benson Italic.
The pictures were done in watercolor and ink.

Candlewick Press
2067 Massachusetts Avenue
Cambridge, Massachusetts 02140

The Tale of the Turnip

BRIAN ALDERSON *illustrated by* FRITZ WEGNER

CANDLEWICK PRESS
CAMBRIDGE, MASSACHUSETTS

*O*nce, a good time ago, there was an old farmer.
He lived in a ramshackle cottage, with a few chickens
and suchlike, and he looked after a few fields.

*But just across the way there was an arrogant old squire.
He lived in a great swanky house, with stables and gardens,
and fields and meadows, and chickens and pigs, and cows
and horses, and who knows what else.*

*N*ow one day the old farmer went
out into his fields and planted a lot of turnips.

*S*ome of them grew and some of them didn't.

But right bang in the middle of one field, there was a turnip that grew . . .

and grew . . .

and grew . . .

and grew ...

and grew.

"Hen's teeth!" said the old farmer to his missus. "This is a right champion turnip. We must take it to the king." So they got a block and tackle, and they heaved it up out of the ground and onto a wagon . . .

and they took it to the king.

"*Stone the crows!*" said the king. "*That's the most champion turnip I ever did see.*"

*H*e gave the old farmer a cartload of gold
and the old farmer went home happy.

When the squire heard about this,
he was furious. "What!—What!—What!" he shouted.
"Giving that old codger a cartload of gold for a miserable turnip!
Why, I've got a stable full of horses out there, and any one of 'em's
worth a thousand turnips. I'll give the king one of those."

So he fetched out his best horse, put it in the wagon so as not to wear it out, and he took it to give to the king.

"By gum!" said the king. "That's the most gussied-up horse I ever did see. Why, not even the crown jewels are a fit reward for a horse like that. What'll I give you?... I know ... you can have ...

my champion turnip!"